'There are no days like the good old days.'
Krazy Kat Comic

JEREMIAH
IN THE
DARK WOODS

Janet and Allan Ahlberg

PUFFIN BOOKS

PUFFIN BOOKS

Published by the Penguin Group
27 Wrights Lane, London W8 5TZ, England
Viking Penguin Inc., 40 West 23rd Street, New York, New York 10010, USA
Penguin Books Australia Ltd, Ringwood, Victoria, Australia
Penguin Books Canada Ltd, 2801 John Street, Markham, Ontario, Canada L3R 1B4
Penguin Books (NZ) Ltd, 182–190 Wairau Road, Auckland 10, New Zealand

Penguin Books Ltd, Registered Offices: Harmondsworth, Middlesex, England

First published by Kestrel Books 1977
Published in Puffin Books 1989
1 3 5 7 9 10 8 6 4 2

Filmset in Plantin

Made and printed in Great Britain by William Clowes Limited,
Beccles and London

Once upon a time there were three bears, seven dwarfs, five gorillas, a frog prince, some sleeping beauties, a wolf, a dinosaur, a Mad Hatter, a steamboat, four firemen on a fire-engine, a crocodile with a clock in it, a considerable number of giant beanstalks – and a little boy named Jeremiah Obadiah Jackenory Jones.

Jeremiah Obadiah Jackenory Jones lived with his grandma in the middle of the Dark Woods. Jeremiah's grandma's house was made of gingerbread and cakes, with window-panes of clear sugar and a roof of chocolate fudge. Jeremiah was very happy there. He was fond of his grandma and enjoyed eating the house.

One morning Jeremiah's grandma said, 'Jeremiah, I am going to make some nice jam tarts for your auntie who lives beyond the Dark Woods, across the river, over the hills and a great way off, and I want you to take them to her.'

'Yes, Grandma,' Jeremiah said.

And so Jeremiah's grandma made the tarts and placed them on the window-sill in the kitchen to cool. Jeremiah went up to his room and played with his train-set for a time before getting ready to leave. At nine o'clock he put on his coat, his flat hat and his best walking-boots and came downstairs. At that moment his grandma shouted to him from the kitchen.

'My goodness, Jeremiah, come quick, the tarts have gone!'

Jeremiah ran into the kitchen and saw at once the terrible empty space on the window-sill. The tarts had gone; nor was that all – the plate had gone too.

Now Jeremiah's grandma was the cleverest and bravest lady of her age for many miles around. She

6

could add up numbers faster than a blink, climb trees like a squirrel and fight wolves and crocodiles with her bare hands and a handbag, when she had to. But her strength was mostly in her arms; she wasn't good at walking and she couldn't really run at all.

'Jeremiah,' said his grandma, 'somewhere out in the Dark Woods there is the no-good robber who has taken your auntie's tarts. I want you to go and get him, Jeremiah!'

'Yes, Grandma,' Jeremiah said.

After this he gave his grandma a little kiss and the wallpaper a little lick, for it was made of peppermint candy, and climbed out through the kitchen window to follow the trail of blurry-looking footprints that led across the garden and away into the trees.

Beneath the trees, however, these footprints soon disappeared in the dry leaves which covered the ground. But Jeremiah did not give up.

'I will keep looking for that robber till I find him,' he said.

He walked on, crunching the leaves with his best boots and humming a little tune to himself to fill up the silence.

When he had gone some distance from the house Jeremiah saw three bears coming towards him – a father bear, a mother bear and a baby bear.

'My name is Jeremiah Obadiah Jackenory Jones,' Jeremiah said, 'and I am looking for the no-good robber who has taken my auntie's tarts.'

'Don't look at us,' said the father bear; 'we only eat porridge.'

'Which we are going home to eat right now,' the

mother bear said. 'We just came out for a little walk while it was cooling.'

'My grandma lost my auntie's tarts while they were cooling,' Jeremiah said.

'Your grandma is a good grandma, I am sure,' said the father bear. 'But those persons who take tarts from old ladies may well think twice before stealing porridge from a bear.'

'Or from two bears,' said the mother bear.

'Or from three bears!' the baby bear said.

'Anyone who takes tarts from my grandma could make a rug out of a bear if he really wanted to,' Jeremiah said.

After this Jeremiah raised his hat to the bears, said 'Goodbye' to them and went on his way.

But he had taken only a few steps when he came upon five gorillas sitting round a table, playing cards and drinking bottles of beer.

Jeremiah began to speak. 'My name is Jeremiah Oba-'

'We know what your name is,' said one of the gorillas. 'Heard you talking to them bears.'

Jeremiah tried to continue. 'I am looking for –'

'Heard that as well,' said the same gorilla. 'And what I have to tell you is, we have seen no tarts whatsoever – isn't that a fact, friends?'

The other gorillas said, yes it was a fact most definitely it was.

'Also, all of us have the perfect alibi that we have been sitting here on this very spot, playing cards and drinking beer, since Tuesday – what day is it today?'

'Friday,' Jeremiah said.

'So there you are,' the gorilla said. 'Now, if you will excuse us, friend, we will get on with the game. You see, in just a little while we have a boat to catch.'

Then, with a cheerful wave to Jeremiah, the gorilla who had done most of the talking turned to the one sitting on his left and said, 'Deal.'

Jeremiah went on his way. Soon he was playing a game of his own where he had to step between the little patches of sunlight which were scattered on the ground. If he trod on the sunlight that would be bad luck, he said to himself, and he would never see his auntie's tarts again.

The next person Jeremiah met was a wolf. This wolf had on a pair of overalls and was doing repairs to a motor-cycle which was upside down on the ground, surrounded by tools and bits and pieces of machinery.

'My name is Jeremiah Obadiah Jackenory Jones,' Jeremiah said, 'and I am looking for the no-good robber who has taken my auntie's tarts.'

'Not guilty,' said the wolf and he wiped a smudge of oil from his face with a rag. 'I only eat grandmas myself.'

Then the wolf looked hard at Jeremiah and said, 'Have you got a grandma, boy?'

'Yes, I've got a grandma,' Jeremiah said, 'and she can fight wolves like you with her bare hands and a handbag, when she has to.'

'Oh,' said the wolf, 'I think I may have heard about her.' And with a crafty smile at Jeremiah, he took up a wrench and went back to the repairing of his motor-cycle.

By this time Jeremiah was feeling tired. When he had put some distance between himself and the wolf, therefore, he sat down under a tree and rested for a while.

Jeremiah leaned back against the cool trunk of the tree and thought about the mystery of his auntie's tarts. The wolf didn't have them, although he couldn't really trust that wolf; the gorillas didn't have them – they hadn't been anywhere since Tuesday, and the bears didn't have them.

At that moment the bears themselves – all three of them – came running past, looking very hot and angry. As they went by they shouted something to Jeremiah about stolen porridge and broken chairs, but before he could reply they had disappeared again into the trees.

Jeremiah got to his feet, brushed himself down, undid the buttons of his coat – he also was feeling warm now, and went on his way.

When Jeremiah met the dinosaur he did not know at first that he had done so; for the dinosaur's back legs were like the trunks of trees and the rest of its body was hidden away by the thick covering of branches and leaves overhead. But then Jeremiah saw the dinosaur's head come swooping down towards him on the end of its long neck, and he heard the dinosaur say:

'"Oh for the good old days, them good old days as is gone for ever – dashash it!"'

Jeremiah could see now that the dinosaur was holding a Krazy Kat comic in one of its paws, from which, presumably, it had been reading.

'My name is Jeremiah Obadiah Jackenory Jones,' Jeremiah said.

'That is just too much name for so short a boy, in my opinion,' the dinosaur said.

'I am looking for the no-good robber who has taken my auntie's tarts,' Jeremiah said.

'Well, I wish you luck in the search,' the dinosaur said; 'although robbers and tarts, in my opinion, are not easy things to find.'

The dinosaur began to withdraw its head back to a position above the trees. 'Come to think of it, though, I saw a fellow back there just now; he was eating something. Might have been tarts, then again might have been turkey pie, you never can tell.'

As Jeremiah set off in the direction the dinosaur had suggested, he noticed its tree-trunk legs begin to walk away and heard its deep, melodious voice reading again in the invisible space above his head:

'"Them was the days, the dear days, the fair days, the rare days, the old, old days for ever gone – golding it!"'

And Jeremiah thought to himself, 'Aren't these the good old days? I always thought they were.'

Jeremiah went on his way until he came to a house with a roof that seemed to be thatched with fur and chimneys that were shaped like the ears of a rabbit. A table was set out under a tree in front of the house and a person, whom Jeremiah recognized as the Mad Hatter, was sitting there all alone. The Hatter had a half-eaten sandwich in one hand and a watch in the other, which he was shaking every now and then and holding to his ear.

When he saw Jeremiah coming the Hatter shouted, 'No room, no room!'

'There's plenty of room,' Jeremiah said and he sat down in a large armchair at one end of the table. This armchair felt warm to Jeremiah, as though, perhaps, somebody had been sitting there not very long ago.

The Hatter was still shaking the watch and holding it to his ear.

'What day is it?' he said.

'Friday,' Jeremiah said.

'Can't you do better than that?' said the Hatter.

So Jeremiah said, 'Wednesday.'

'That's better,' said the Hatter.

'Tuesday?' Jeremiah said.

'Better still,' said the Hatter.

'Monday!' shouted Jeremiah.

'Perfect!' said the Hatter. 'Have some more tea.' He leaned forward and raised the lid of the teapot. 'Sorry, I was forgetting – it's got a dormouse in there.' And he slammed the lid back into place.

Jeremiah next spoke to the Mad Hatter about his auntie's tarts and the no-good robber who had taken them.

And the Hatter said, 'The story *I* hear is that the Queen has lost some tarts also. Could be we have an outbreak of tart-taking going on.'

At that moment a dark shadow fell across the table.

'Save us!' shouted the Hatter. 'It is the dragon!' He leapt up from his chair and, with the teapot tucked under his arm, ran off in the direction of the house.

'It is no dragon,' said a deep, melodious voice. 'It is I!' And then the dinosaur's head appeared, coming right up close to Jeremiah across the table. 'That was the fellow I was telling you about,' said the dinosaur and he pointed after the fleeing Hatter who was just at that moment entering the house and banging the door behind him. 'Any luck with the tarts?'

'No,' Jeremiah said. He picked up the half-eaten sandwich which the Hatter in his haste had left behind. 'It was a sandwich he was eating.'

'A turkey sandwich?' said the dinosaur.

Jeremiah opened the sandwich. 'No, fish paste,' he said.

After this the dinosaur withdrew his head once more into the trees. Jeremiah got up from the table, waved to the Hatter whose face he could see pressed to one of the upstairs windows of the house, and went on his way.

When Jeremiah reached the river he found a large crocodile stretched out upon the bank. This crocodile was cleaning its teeth with a toothbrush and smiling at itself from time to time in a small silver mirror.

'My name is Jeremiah Obadiah Jackenory Jones,' Jeremiah said.

'That's nice,' said the crocodile. It turned away from its mirror and gave Jeremiah a big smile.

'I am looking for the no-good robber who has taken my auntie's tarts,' Jeremiah said.

A thoughtful expression now appeared on the crocodile's face. 'Would these be *jam* tarts?' it said.

'Yes,' Jeremiah said.

'By any chance would this jam be *strawberry* jam, all dark and delicious from the baking?'

'Yes,' Jeremiah said.

'And is it possible that the pastry of these tarts is a golden brown with glorious little crisp and curly edges?'

'Yes!' Jeremiah said.

'Then you have come to the right place,' said the crocodile; 'for I am most familiar with confectionery of this description. Come and sit beside me here and we will discuss the matter.'

But Jeremiah did no such thing; he knew all about crocodiles. Instead he said, 'What is that ticking sound I can hear?'

'It is me,' said the crocodile. 'There was a time in my youth when I mistakenly swallowed a clock.' Once more the crocodile smiled invitingly at Jeremiah. 'Now, if you would care to come and sit beside me, you might hear it the better.' And added, 'It has been known to chime, you know, on special occasions.'

At that moment a fire-engine burst upon the scene. It was skidding and swerving between the trees, throwing up clouds of dust, and its bell was ringing furiously.

'Which way's the fire?' shouted the firemen.

There were four of them altogether.

'That way,' said the crocodile, pointing lazily back into the trees.

With more clangings of its bell, the fire-engine swung round and collided with a tree, causing one of the

firemen to lose his hat. Then it shot off again as rapidly as it had arrived.

When it had gone Jeremiah said, 'Is there really a fire that way?'

'Not that I know of,' said the crocodile. 'Now, with regard to this clock of mine we were talking about.'

But even as the crocodile was speaking, a small dusty figure in an enormous hat came hurrying towards them. It was the Mad Hatter again.

'Was that a fire-engine that I heard?' he said.

'Yes,' Jeremiah said.

'Good,' said the Hatter. 'That's what we need – fire-engines!'

'Are you connected with a fire then, sir, may I ask?' said the crocodile.

'Not exactly,' said the Hatter. He took off his hat and blew a little dust from its flat surface. 'I have been having some trouble recently with a dragon.'

'No, it was a dinosaur,' Jeremiah said.

'Who told you that?' said the Hatter.

'The dinosaur told me,' Jeremiah said.

'Then it was a dragon for sure,' said the Hatter; 'for dragons, it is well-known, will lie their socks off when they have to. Whereas dinosaurs, on the other hand, are the most truthful creatures ever to trample on the earth!' The Hatter put his hat back on and patted it firmly into place. 'Well, dragons, of course, have this other bad habit of breathing smoke and flames everywhere, which is a thing I do not like.'

'Ah,' said the crocodile, 'so you called the fire-engine to put it out!'

'Yes, I did,' said the Hatter.

'That is good thinking, sir, if you will allow me to say so,' said the crocodile, and it smiled invitingly at the Hatter. 'Now I myself have had some experience with dragons which, if you'd care to come and sit beside me here, I would be most happy to tell you about.'

But the Mad Hatter did no such thing; he wasn't as mad as all that.

Jeremiah left the crocodile and the Mad Hatter and set off along the river bank to the place where he believed there was a bridge. But it was now the middle of the day and Jeremiah was feeling hungry. When he had put some distance between himself and the crocodile, therefore, he sat down under a small peach tree and helped himself to some of the red and golden fruit which was hanging there. After this he took off his best boots and socks and rolled up his trousers to the knee so that he might cool his feet in the river.

As Jeremiah looked down at his own toes rippling and wriggling beneath the glass-green water, he thought again about the mystery of his auntie's tarts. The crocodile didn't have them, although he couldn't really trust that crocodile; the dinosaur didn't have them – he could trust the dinosaur, and the Mad Hatter didn't have them. Also, from what the Hatter had said, it seemed as though the Queen didn't have them either – she didn't even have her own tarts any more.

At that moment a brightly-painted steamboat, with little puffs of grey smoke rising from its funnel, came chugging round the bend of the river. Beside the wheel-house on the upper deck a man in naval uniform was standing, holding a megaphone. Next to the man, and clinging tightly to his free arm, stood a lady in a flowery dress with a handkerchief held up to her eyes.

'Ahoy there!' said the man.

'Ahoy there!' Jeremiah said.

'Our names are Captain and Mrs Dawkins,' said the man, 'and we are presently in search of our daughter, Miss Margery Daw Dawkins, otherwise known as "Goldilocks" on account of her beautiful long and golden hair. She has been missing these fifteen hours and we are inconsolable without her.'

'What does "inconsolable" mean?' Jeremiah said.

'It means that we are very sad,' said the Captain.

The steamboat had gone past Jeremiah by this time, and the Captain and his wife were walking along the starboard side towards the stern.

'I have not seen your daughter, Captain Dawkins,' Jeremiah said. 'But should I do so, I will rescue her and send you word.'

'Thank you, my boy,' the Captain said. 'You will be a gentleman in future years, I can see that.'

Mrs Dawkins now tried to speak to Jeremiah but was overcome by the sadness of the occasion and succeeded only in sobbing loudly down the megaphone.

Finally, as the boat approached a further bend in the river, Jeremiah noticed the five gorillas he had met earlier. They were sitting in the stern under a striped canvas sunshade, playing cards and drinking bottles of

beer just as before. One of the gorillas got to his feet, took off his hat and waved.

'Ahoy there, Jeremiah Obadiah Jackenory Jones!' he said.

'Ahoy there!' Jeremiah said.

Then the other gorillas took off their hats and waved, and Jeremiah waved too and kept on waving, while the little puffs of smoke from the boat's funnel rose up into the blue sky like Indian signals, and the boat itself passed out of sight.

When he had dried his feet with his handkerchief, Jeremiah put on his socks and boots again and filled the pockets of his coat with peaches. There was no shortage of fruit in the Dark Woods; peaches and oranges, cherries and plums, breadfruits even, all grew there and could be found by people who knew where to look. But Jeremiah expected to be crossing the river soon and leaving the woods behind. Fruit trees were less plentiful on the other side, he had heard, and so he took the peaches.

Jeremiah went on his way, whistling a little tune to himself and pausing now and then to skim a stone or two across the water. After a time he came to an iron bridge decorated along its sides with iron roses and guarded at each end by pairs of iron dogs. Jeremiah stepped onto the bridge and saw at once that it was occupied. There, sitting on the handrail, with its little feet dangling over the side, was a young-looking frog. This frog had a tiny crown on its head and was holding a fishing-rod out over the water. Jeremiah approached the frog.

'My name is Jeremiah Obadiah Jackenory Jones,' he said.

'So what?' said the frog. '*My* name is Horatio Malvolio Gladiolo Dunbar D'Arcy FitzHenry the Fourth!'

'I am looking for the no-good robber who has taken my auntie's tarts,' Jeremiah said.

'Why ask me?' said the frog. 'Do I look like I would be eating tarts? Anyway, I am not some no-good robber – I am a prince! Besides all that, I never met your auntie.'

Suddenly the frog leaned back and heaved violently on his fishing-rod.

'A bite,' he said, 'I've got a bite!'

A small brown fish came up out of the water on the end of the line. Frantically, the frog reached out to grab it. Before he could do so, however, the fish said, 'Good afternoon, nice day,' and by opening its mouth to speak in this fashion it let go of the line and plopped back into the water.

Good afternoon, nice day

'Blast it!' said the frog. He stared angrily at Jeremiah. 'That was your fault – you put me off!'

'I did no such thing,' Jeremiah said, and he began to walk away from the frog towards the other end of the bridge.

'Wait a minute,' said the frog. 'Where are you going?' He picked up a little tin of worms and swung the rod and line over his shoulder. 'Never mind, I'll walk along with you for a while.'

Beyond the bridge there was an ornamental garden full of floral clocks and fountains, elaborately patterned flowerbeds and birds and insects of every description.

As Jeremiah and the frog strolled through the garden, the frog apologized for his bad temper.

'I am upset somewhat from having been turned into a frog like this,' he said.

'I can understand that,' Jeremiah said. 'How did it happen?'

'Oh, it was a malicious fairy,' said the frog; 'you know the kind. She didn't like me for some reason or other, and turned me into a frog. Now the only hope I have of becoming a prince again is if some princess kisses me.' The frog kicked moodily at the gravel path. 'Fat chance of that!'

'Are there no princesses then, hereabouts?' Jeremiah said.

'Oh, there are princesses,' said the frog. 'Trouble is, most of them wouldn't kiss a frog if you paid them. Then again, princesses have problems of their own, being locked up in high towers by ogres and that kind of thing; also being sent fast asleep for hundreds of years at a time till some prince comes along and kisses *them!*'

'Like Sleeping Beauty, you mean,' Jeremiah said.

'That's it,' said the frog. 'Though some of them are not that beautiful, if you ask me.' He picked up a little stone from the path and threw it in the air. 'There's one of them in here, you know.'

'What – a sleeping beauty?' Jeremiah said.

'Yes, just over there.'

The frog waved his fishing-rod in the direction of a small alabaster pavilion. This pavilion was glittering in the sunlight and shimmering also in the way buildings sometimes do when they have a spell on them.

Then the frog said, 'Come and take a look.'

Inside the pavilion Jeremiah found a great many cobwebs, a half-empty pop bottle with a straw in it and a long glass box inside which a young woman was sleeping.

'That's her,' said the frog; 'been there forty-five years, so they say.'

Jeremiah leaned over the box. 'She looks very peaceful,' he said.

'So would you,' said the frog, 'if you'd been sleeping all that time. It's not like being turned into a frog, you know. That's where the real aggravation is – ask anybody!'

When Jeremiah and the frog had left the pavilion and returned to the path, the frog said, 'I'm going to leave you now. There is a story going round that the seven dwarfs have a girl staying with them – name of Snow White. Well, you know how it is, some people are saying she is really a princess, and I have been thinking for a day or two I should go over there and look into the matter. Of course, with my luck she'll turn out not to be a princess at all; or, if she is, some witch will have been there first and put *her* to sleep.'

'Or changed her into a frog, perhaps,' Jeremiah said.

'Oh, don't say that,' said the frog.

At that moment the three bears came racing out of a nearby shrubbery and charged across the path in front of Jeremiah and the frog.

'Did you see her?' said the father bear. He was looking hotter and angrier than ever.

'Who?' Jeremiah said.

'That no-good, low-down, female porridge-stealer!' said the father bear.

But then, before Jeremiah could reply, the bears were off again, grunting and growling across the grass before disappearing once more among the beech trees and rhododendron bushes on the other side of the garden.

'Those bears are a long way from home,' said the frog.
'Yes,' Jeremiah said; and after he had parted company
with the frog he thought to himself, 'So am I.'

Jeremiah left the garden and followed the road that led
up from the bridge, away from the river, over the hills
and a great way off. By three o'clock he had passed the
Brick Works and the old Botanical Gardens and come to
a place where giant beanstalks grew up into the sky. By

four o'clock he had climbed the first of the hills and could see the Ghost Town, half-hidden in mist as usual, spread out below him. By five o'clock he was approaching a grove of pepper trees with clouds of parakeets and finches flying above it. And by half-past five he was resting once more and eating peaches beneath a high tower around which there was a little moat. Jeremiah had some hope of meeting a princess at this time, or an ogre even, and questioning them about his auntie's tarts – but the tower was deserted.

When he had finished his peaches, Jeremiah took a tobacco tin lid which he had found in the grass and went to sail it on the moat. If the lid sank that would be bad luck, he said to himself, and he would never see his auntie's tarts again.

At that moment a motor-cyclist came riding up over the brow of the hill. He stopped, dismounted and removed his crash-helmet. Jeremiah saw it was the wolf.

'I forgot to ask you, boy,' said the wolf. 'Is there a reward?'

'For finding the tarts?' Jeremiah said.

'Yes,' said the wolf.

'No,' Jeremiah said.

'Oh,' said the wolf.

He stood for a moment looking down into the moat and also sideways at Jeremiah. Then he whistled a chorus of, 'Who's Afraid of the Big Bad Wolf', put his helmet back on and returned to his motor-cycle.

'Well, I'm going. I have to see this little girl about her grandma.' The wolf smiled craftily at Jeremiah. 'You know how it is.'

Jeremiah lay back in the warm grass and yawned. The sounds of the departing motor-cycle went echoing down into the next valley and faded gradually away. Jeremiah closed his eyes and yawned again, turned over on his side, day-dreamed for a time about various things and, finally, fell asleep.

When Jeremiah awoke, the moon and stars were shining overhead, fire-flies were glowing in the darkness of the surrounding trees, and the ground was shaking.

'Goodness,' Jeremiah said, 'it is an earthquake!'

He buttoned up his coat and pulled his flat hat more firmly into place. Then, suddenly, the moon was blotted out by an enormous head and neck, and a voice said:

'It is no earthquake – it is I!'

The dinosaur stretched himself out full-length along the side of the hill. In this position he no longer hid the moon, and Jeremiah could see that he was carrying a passenger. It was a little girl with a pale face, bright eyes and long golden hair.

'Jeremiah,' said the dinosaur, 'it is late; long past the time when a person of your age and size should be in bed, in my opinion.'

'But I am looking for the no-good robber who has taken my auntie's tarts!' Jeremiah said.

'Forget the tarts, Jeremiah,' said the dinosaur. 'They are for ever gone – believe me.'

'What about the robber?' Jeremiah said.

The dinosaur shook his head sadly. 'There was no robber, Jeremiah,' he said; 'only a poor and hungry little person –'

'I was starving!' shouted the girl.

'– separated from the affections of her loving parents –'

'I fell off the boat!' shouted the girl. 'And got left behind – I was soaked!'

'– lost in the Dark Woods, a stranger in a strange land –'

'I didn't know where I was!' shouted the girl.

'Wait a minute,' Jeremiah said. 'Did she take the tarts?'

'She took them, Jeremiah,' said the dinosaur. 'Her name is Goldilocks.'

Then Goldilocks shouted down to Jeremiah about how the dinosaur had rescued her from the three bears.

'He just picked me up like I was a little flower for his buttonhole!' she said. 'And so fast, I bet them bears never even knew I was gone!'

And the dinosaur said, 'Oh, it was nothing – any dinosaur would have done the same, in my opinion.'

'Wait a minute,' Jeremiah said. 'Did she take the porridge as well?'

'She took it, Jeremiah,' said the dinosaur; 'in a moment of weakness –'

'I had to break the door down!' Goldilocks said.

'– and having just finished off the tarts.'

Then the dinosaur said, 'But come, Jeremiah, all that is history now. Climb aboard and we will deliver Goldilocks once more into her father's boat. After which I will return you to your grandma.'

And so Jeremiah rode home with Goldilocks on the dinosaur and thought for the last time about the mystery of his auntie's tarts. It was solved now, of course, and yet there was just one thing that was bothering him. When they came to the river and could see the lights of the steamboat shining below, Jeremiah tapped Goldilocks on the shoulder and said, 'What did you do with the plate?'

'I kept it,' Goldilocks said. 'Only then I had to throw it at those bears – they were going to eat me!'

'No, they only eat porridge,' Jeremiah said.

'Well, I was more or less full of porridge at the time,' Goldilocks said. Then she said, 'Oh, look – there's my mum and dad!'

Now the dinosaur stepped out into the river and lowered his head so that it lay alongside the steamboat. Goldilocks climbed up over his ears, down between his eyes and along his nose until she was able to jump onto the deck and into her mother's arms.

After this Captain Dawkins raised his megaphone and thanked Jeremiah and the dinosaur, on behalf of himself and his wife, for finding their beloved Goldilocks. Mrs Dawkins also tried to say a few words but was unable to do so, being overcome by the happiness of the occasion.

'Oh, I didn't do anything,' Jeremiah said. 'It was the dinosaur.'

'Not at all, not at all,' the dinosaur said. 'And besides, any dinosaur would have done the same, in my opinion.'

'I didn't know there were any other dinosaurs,' Captain Dawkins said.

'True,' said the dinosaur, 'very true.' But then he added quietly, so that only Jeremiah heard, 'Yet I do believe there were hundreds of us, thousands of us even . . . in the good old days.'

Jeremiah rode home on the dinosaur through the Dark Woods. At last he came to his grandma's garden, with the trail of blurry-looking footprints still leading to and from the kitchen window, and his grandma's house, with its walls of gingerbread and cakes sparkling in the moonlight.

Jeremiah's grandma was standing on the front step, waiting to greet him.

'My goodness, Jeremiah,' she said, 'is *that* the no-good robber who has taken your auntie's tarts?'

'No, Grandma,' Jeremiah said. 'It is the dinosaur.'

'Ah, yes,' said his grandma. 'My eyes are not so good in this moonlight. I thought at first it was a dragon you had there.'

Then Jeremiah's grandma and the dinosaur said, 'How do you do?' and 'Pleased to meet you' to each other, and Jeremiah told his grandma all that had happened to him during the day.

When he spoke of the sleeping beauty his grandma said, 'Goodness, is that one still there? She must be older than I am!' When he mentioned the wolf she said, 'Yes, I think I may have heard about him.' And when he had finished she said, 'So it was Goldilocks – who would have believed it? It makes you wonder what young girls are coming to these days.'

'Yes, Grandma,' Jeremiah said and he gave the door-knocker a little lick. It was made of treacle toffee.

'Well, Jeremiah,' said grandma, 'you are a good boy and a brave one; also, in this dinosaur I do believe you have discovered a true friend. Are you hungry?'

'Yes, Grandma,' Jeremiah said. He was licking the door itself now. It was made of barley-sugar and seaside rock.

'Are *you* hungry?' said his grandma to the dinosaur. But then, before the dinosaur could reply, she said, 'Oh, of course you are – a big fellow like you!'

After this she squeezed past Jeremiah and disappeared into the house. When she returned she was carrying an enormous plate.

'I always knew you'd find the robber, Jeremiah,' said his grandma. 'But I must confess, I thought the tarts themselves would be for ever gone. And so – as you can see – I made some more!'

Jeremiah looked at the enormous plate piled high with tarts, each one a little cup of golden pastry with glorious crisp and curly edges, full to the brim with strawberry jam all dark and delicious from the baking.

The dinosaur looked at the tarts also, and he said, 'Those are the finest-looking tarts that I have ever seen in my life, ma'am.'

'But what about the good old days?' Jeremiah said. 'Didn't they have better tarts then?'

'Not at all,' said the dinosaur. 'Those were the bad old days, in my opinion, as far as tarts were concerned.'

Jeremiah and his grandma sat down on the front step, the dinosaur stretched himself out on the ground and together they began to eat the tarts.